GILL GRUNT
AND THE CURSE OF
THE FISH MASTER

Published by Puffin 2013
A Penguin Company
Penguin Books Ltd, 80 Strand, London, WC2R 0RL, UK
Penguin Group (USA) Inc., 375 Hudson Street, New York 10014, USA
Penguin Books Australia Ltd, 707 Collins Street, Melbourne, Victoria 3008,
Australia (A division of Pearson Australia Group Pty Ltd)
Canada, India, New Zealand, South Africa

Written by Cavan Scott
Illustrated by Dani Geremia – Beehive Illustration Agency

www.puffinbooks.com

ISBN: 978-1-40939-199-9
004
Printed in Great Britain

ALWAYS LEARNING

PEARSON

GILL GRUNT
AND THE CURSE OF
THE FISH MASTER

by Onk Beakman

PUFFIN

CONTENTS

ABOUT THE AUTHOR

Onk Beakman knew he wanted to be a world-famous author from the moment he was hatched. In fact, the book-loving penguin was so keen that he wrote his first novel while still inside his egg (to this day, nobody is entirely sure where he got the tiny pencil and notebook from).

Growing up on the icy wastes of Skylands' Frozen Desert was difficult for a penguin who hated the cold. While his brothers plunged into the freezing waters, Onk could be found with his beak buried in a book and a pen clutched in his flippers.

Yet his life changed forever when a giant floating head appeared in the skies above the tundra. It was Kaos, attempting to melt the icecaps so he could get his grubby little hands on an ancient weapon buried beneath the snow.

Onk watched open-beaked as Spyro swept in and sent the evil Portal Master packing. From that day, Onk knew that he must chronicle the Skylanders' greatest adventures. He travelled the length and breadth of Skylands, collecting every tale he could find about Master Eon's brave champions.

Today, Onk writes from a shack on the beautiful sands of Blistering Beach with his two pet sea cucumbers.

CHAPTER ONE

GUT-ROT, THE PIRATE CHEF

For as long as anyone can remember, and maybe even a bit longer than that, pirates have terrorized the magical realm of Skylands. They plunder and pilfer here, there and everywhere, raiding villages, stealing treasure and leaving chaos in their wake. They do what they please and don't care what you think about it.

However, contrary to popular opinion, a pirate's life isn't all fun, laughter and yo-ho-ho-ing from dawn to dusk. Yes, most enjoy the plundering and pilfering, and the raiding and treasure bits aren't bad either, but there is one drawback to being a pirate. The food is disgusting. Your average pirate meal consists of sheep wool porridge, followed by sheep wool biscuits and rounded off by a generous helping of sheep wool surprise dessert. The surprise is that the dessert isn't made of sheep wool at all. It is made from raw onion and drenched in mud gravy.

The problem is that most pirate chefs don't actually like cooking. They'd rather be plundering and pilfering than messing around in the kitchen. That is, except for Gut-Rot, chief chef of the Fearsome Fang.

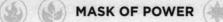
The Fearsome Fang was a ship to be, well, feared. If you spotted it approaching, your best course of action was to run away. Very fast. No, faster than that. The pirates of the Fearsome Fang were the toughest bunch of buccaneers you'd ever have the misfortune to meet. Pirates everywhere dreamt of serving on-board the Fearsome Fang beneath her captain, the infamous Captain Grimslobber. Grimslobber was so good at pirating that he didn't just have one wooden leg; he had two. He didn't just have one gold tooth; he had a mouthful. He even didn't just have one parrot; he had an entire flock. Gut-Rot knew it was

an honour to serve such a legendary captain. Because of this, he wasn't content to just serve up the usual sheep wool muck. He wanted to be different. He wanted to produce the finest pirate cuisine possible.

There were only two problems with all this. First up, Gut-Rot couldn't cook. He thought he could, but his food was so appalling that the crew of the Fearsome Fang longed for sheep wool porridge.

Secondly, Gut-Rot had lost his taste buds in a game of Skystones years ago and so couldn't even taste how bad his grub actually was. He just assumed it was delicious.

One day Gut-Rot decided to make crab ice-cream sundaes with seafood wafers. Can you think of anything grosser than fish-flavoured ice-cream? Yet Gut-Rot toiled all morning and was just about to add the final ingredient – the crabs themselves.

Wiping his hands on his stained apron, Gut-

Rot approached the larder where the barrels of crabs were kept. This was going to be his greatest triumph yet; a meal that would be talked about for years to come. However, as he drew nearer the barrels he paused. He could hear knocking. Was it someone at the galley door? No, it was coming from the barrels. From *inside* the barrels. It sounded as if the crabs were trying to get out.

But that was ridiculous.

Wasn't it?

The barrel at the top of the pile shuddered. The knocking got louder and louder, the sound of hundreds of tiny claws scraping against the wooden lid becoming unbearable.

Suddenly, the barrel lurched forward and smashed into the floor, seawater and snapping white crabs splashing everywhere.

"Bilious Barnacles!" shrieked Gut-Rot. "Supper will be ruined – ruined, I tells ye!"

Gut-Rot reached for a broom, but froze when

he felt hundreds of beady little eyes on his back. He turned slowly, gasping as he realized that every single crab in the galley was standing looking straight at him.

Instinctively, he took a step back. The crabs took a step forward. He gulped and took another step back. The crabs followed. He raised the broom as a warning. The crabs raised their claws. This time, Gut-Rot did more than gulp. As the crabs began surging towards him, he screamed and ran.

The crew of The Fearsome Fang looked up from their chores as the door to the galley flew open and Gut-Rot charged out onto the deck. He was screaming. He was shouting. He was covered in snapping white crabs from head to foot.

"Aaaaaaargh!" he yelled, trying to pluck a crab from his eyebrow. "They be after me! 'Undreds of 'em!"

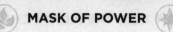
Sure enough, hundreds of crabs flowed out of the galley, chasing after Gut-Rot, following his every step. Worryingly, some even carried all manner of kitchen knives in their claws. Bread knives, carving knives, vicious looking cleavers, all waved in Gut-Rot's general direction.

Beside himself with fear, Gut-Rot made for the ship's plank. Screaming at the top of his voice, he raced along its length and, in a final bid to escape the rampaging crustaceans, threw himself overboard, plunging into the clouds below.

As one, the mob of angry crabs streamed after him, kitchen utensils glinting in the sunshine. Without stopping, every last one of them raced off the plank and plummeted after their quarry. Soon, there wasn't a single crab left on the Fearsome Fang.

The crew looked at each other in bewilderment. What had they just witnessed? Had Gut-Rot really been chased off the ship by their supper?

Behind them a door opened and Captain Grimslobber stepped onto the deck, at least four parrots on each shoulder. He strode over to the side of the ship and peered overboard, watching his chef tumble away followed by the mass of snapping crabs.

"That be a shame," he said, turning back to his crew. "A real pity, truth be told." Grimslobber's face broke into a nasty, golden smile. "Ah well mateys. Anyone for takeout?"

CHAPTER TWO

OPENING THE BOOK OF POWER

Gill Grunt loved being a Skylander. Why wouldn't he? He was the only Gillman who had ever been invited to join the courageous band of heroes who had pledged to protect Skylands from danger. Also, it meant that Gill had travelled to hundreds, no thousands, of the floating islands that made up this magical realm. From the moment he was born, Gill had loved to explore. The great thing about Skylands was that you never ran out of new places to go. No one knew how many islands there were in Skylands. In fact, Spyro, Gill's best friend, had told him that there were an infinite number of islands floating in Skylands' endless blue sky. Some were peaceful and calm, others were wild and perilous, but all brought adventure.

But even that wasn't the best thing about being a Skylander. The best thing was his friends. Gill was always happiest when he was jumping into action with his fellow Skylanders, sharing adventures and working together.

Take today, for example. Today, the Skylanders had been working hard to rebuild the Eternal Archive after it had been attacked by Kaos, the evil (and distinctly smelly) Portal Master who was always trying to take over Skylands. The guy never stopped. He never even took a day's holiday. No matter how many times the Skylanders defeated him, the bald twerp came back with yet another diabolical scheme.

Gill looked up at the towering, newly repaired walls of the Eternal Archive. The Archive housed every book that had ever been written. Kaos had wanted to get his stubby little hands on a very special volume, but Spyro had seen him off, helped by Stealth Elf, Trigger Happy and Drill Sergeant. Unfortunately, the Archive itself had taken quite a battering, but the Skylanders had rallied together to patch it up. Gill had to admit that they'd done a pretty good job. He might even compose a song about it. All Gillmen loved to sing. Unfortunately, they were completely unaware that their singing voices sounded like toads gargling slimy seaweed. Toads with bad colds, at that. The problem was that none of Gill's friends had the heart to tell him how dreadful he sounded. They just made their excuses and left as soon as possible.

Standing in the shadow of the Archive, Gill

took a deep breath, ready to burst into song. Bizarrely, his friends began to scatter. Fright Rider, for example, jumped onto the back of his skeleton steed and raced off into the distance. Terrafin gulped and burrowed beneath the ground, while Slam Bam encased himself in a block of ice to muffle the noise. Even Eruptor, who had been happily relaxing in the sun after a hard day's work, suddenly remembered that he had to go and wash his hair. This was particularly odd as Eruptor doesn't have any hair.

Yup, Gill loved his friends, but he couldn't help but find them a little strange at times!

Gill grinned as he saw Spyro bound out of the Eternal Archive. Spyro would listen to his song. Spyro always loved Gill's singing, even if he did have an odd habit of listening with his claws in his ears.

"Hey Spyro," Gill said, clearing his throat. "Listen to this . . ."

"No, Gills," Spyro cut in, his eyes wide with

excitement. "You have to come listen to this. Master Eon is about to open The Book of Power!"

"What's the Book of Power?" Gill asked as he followed his friend down to the secret vault that was housed deep below the Eternal Archives.

Spyro explained as they scampered towards the vault door: "It's what Kaos was trying to steal. Master Eon says the Book of Power is one of the most important books in Skylands history."

"But what makes it so special?"

"You'll see," said Spyro, darting through the door.

Gill couldn't help but be impressed. The vault was huge. Brushed metal walls stretched high above them, three brilliant beams of light shining down from the domed ceiling. Master Eon was standing in the middle of the spotlight talking to Wiggleworth, the chief curator of the Eternal Archive. Wiggleworth was almost as majestic as the vault itself, standing in a gleaming robotic suit of armour. Of course, Gill knew that the real Wiggleworth was actually a tiny bookworm sitting in the heart of the armour.

As the pair approached, Eon turned and smiled. In contrast, Eon's assistant, the loyal but eternally terrified Hugo, wrung his hands in barely disguised panic.

"What's wrong with Hugo this time?" Gill whispered to Spyro, not expecting Eon to overhear. He should have known better. While the Portal Master was unbelievably old, there was nothing wrong with his hearing.

"Hugo is worried, Gill," Eon intoned, stepping aside to reveal a leather bound book on a lectern. "And for good reason."

Gill gasped. "Is that the Book of Power?" he asked in complete awe.

"Y-yes," stammered Hugo, visibly shaking at Eon's feet, "although its full title is The Book of Power and Other Utterly Terrifying Stuff."

"Yes, thank you Hugo," Eon said.

"Volume Three," Hugo added.

Beside Eon, Wiggleworth tilted his robotic head. "Are you sure about this, Eon?"

The Portal Master nodded gravely.

"I'm afraid so, old friend. If Kaos was after the book, the Skylanders need to know everything."

Gill and Spyro exchanged a worried glance. This sounded serious.

Eon turned to face the book and raised a gnarled hand. As if by magic (which of course it was), the heavy leather cover started to creak open by itself. A gust of stale wind rushed out from the yellowing pages, smothering the room in musty-smelling dust. Gill coughed, trying to clear his throat, his eyes watering. Beside him, Spyro gasped. Wiping his eyes, Gill looked up. At first the brittle pages had been blank, but now a picture was forming, drawn by unseen hands. Instantly, Gill recognized what it was – the Core of Light, the ancient monument that kept the Darkness at bay across Skylands. But

as they watched, the image shifted to something unimaginable, something unthinkable. The sketch now showed the Core utterly destroyed, evil-looking clouds swarming over the sky.

"No!" whispered Spyro, not wanting to believe such a dreadful event could ever happen. But the image was already changing. Gill felt his scales crawl. The book was now showing a picture of the most hideous mask he had ever seen.

CHAPTER THREE

THE MASK OF POWER

"**O**h, no," gulped Hugo, hiding behind Eon's robe. "The Mask of Power. I can't bear it."

"What is it?" Gill asked, unable to tear his eyes away from the terrifying picture. The Mask looked like the face of a monster from your worst nightmares. Actually, it looked like the thing that gave the monster from your worst nightmares nightmares. It glared back at them, sharp fangs crammed into its snarling mouth, jagged horns erupting from its forehead. It looked completely and utterly evil.

"The Mask of Power is completely and utterly evil," Eon said. "It was created millennia ago by a guild of Spell Punks." The image on the page changed once more, now showing sketches of eight mischievous Spell Punks huddled around a cauldron.

"But Spell Punks don't usually work together," pointed out Spyro.

"Which is why the Mask is so dangerous. The Spell Punks created it for their king, a follower of the Darkness who wanted to destroy the Core

of Light. Combining their powers, they conjured up the Mask which is said to be able to tap into all known Elements: Fire, Water, Earth, Air, Life, Undead, Magic and Tech." As Eon recited through the Elements, the eight gems set into the ghastly Mask seemed to glow in turn.

"What does it do?" Gill asked, feeling his stomach tighten as the Water gem flared.

"No one knows for sure," Eon replied. "But we know what happened when the King tried on the Mask of Power." In response to his words, the pictures on the page began to shift, displaying scenes Gill had hoped he would never see. The Forest of Life on fire. The oceans boiling away to nothing. Trolls rampaging through every town and village on Skylands. Zombie sheep on a woolly rampage.

"The King was eventually defeated," Eon continued as the unsettling image of the Mask returned to the page, "and the Mask was broken into eight pieces. The Portal Masters of Old hid the fragments inside eight different objects and scattered them across Skylands so they could never be found."

"To make it even more difficult, the objects were the complete opposite to the fragments that they contained," Hugo added, peaking out from behind Eon's robe.

"What do you mean?" asked Spyro.

"The Undead segment was hidden inside something alive, for example," Hugo explained, wiping his glasses on his sleeve, always happy to give a lecture even when he was petrified. "The Portal Masters of Old were clever so-and-sos, you know."

"Not clever enough," Eon said sadly. "A segment of the Mask has been found."

The picture of the Mask split into its eight fragments, seven of the segments fading away to leave a solitary piece. "The Tech segment was disguised as something completely natural," Eon announced. The fragment blurred, transforming before their eyes. "A beautiful flower."

"Wait a minute," Spyro exclaimed. "I've seen that flower!"

Eon nodded as a new picture appeared on the page. Gill frowned. The Book was now showing a picture of Kaos, proudly pinning the flower on his lapel. "Exactly, Spyro. Kaos has somehow stumbled upon the Tech segment of the Mask . . ."

" . . . And he wanted to steal the Book of Power, the only book in creation that can reveal the location of the remaining fragments," said Wiggleworth gravely, his voice crackling over his armour's speaker system. "He is trying to reassemble the Mask of Power. He wants to use it to destroy the Core of Light."

"Then we need to find the other pieces first!" exclaimed Gill, remembering the images of the destroyed Core.

"But how?" asked Spyro.

Eon replied by raising his staff high above the

Book of Power. "Book of Power," he boomed, staring intently at the pages in front of him. "Only a Portal Master can force you to reveal your secrets. I demand you reveal them to me."

Behind him, Hugo squeaked in alarm and grabbed a handful of Eon's robes. "Quick," he squealed, "grab hold of something!"

"Why?" asked Gill, although Hugo didn't get a chance to reply. He didn't need to. Above them, storm clouds began to form near the ceiling, lightning crackling up and down the walls.

"It's a storm!" Spyro shouted.

"But we're indoors," pointed out Gill.

"It doesn't matter," Wiggleworth yelled, struggling to make himself heard as rain began to lash down. "Hugo is right. This could get . . ."

The Curator never completed his sentence. Instead he was plucked from his armoured feet by the tremendous wind that suddenly whipped through the vault. Gill and Spyro were caught up in the tornado and were sent spinning round

and around. All the while, Eon stood in the eye of the storm, his staff held high and Hugo clutching onto his flapping robes for dear life.

"Getting . . . dizzy . . ." Gill yelled, his arms windmilling as he span around, although he knew Spyro wouldn't be able to hear him. What was Eon doing? Couldn't he save them? Couldn't he get them down?

Then, with a flash of blinding light, the storm subsided as quickly as it had started. The wind vanished, and getting down was suddenly no longer an issue. Gill plummeted back to the floor, throwing his arms over his face to try to break his fall. The further he fell, the harder those cold stone floor slabs looked. Luckily, he never hit them. Inches from the floor, Gill jolted to a halt. He looked up to see Spyro, flapping his purple wings. The dragon had grabbed onto the water barrel that Gill always wore on his back.

"Thanks buddy," he gurgled as he was

lowered gently to the floor. Gill knew he could always rely on Spyro.

"I am sorry about the freak weather conditions my friends," Eon said softly. "The Book didn't want to give up its secrets, but I . . ." the Portal Master paused, "persuaded it. This is where the next segment is hidden." The pages displayed the map of an island covered in shimmering blue water.

"I know that place," Spyro said. So did Gill.

"Deep Water Wasteland," he whispered. This wasn't good. The Wastelands was among the most dangerous seas in all of Skylands. Eon turned to face the Gillman.

"Gill, you know the Wastelands better than any Skylander. Will you go and find the Water segment of the Mask?"

Gill nodded. Of course he would. Anything to stop Kaos. "What is it disguised as?"

"I'm afraid the Book does not know, but this will help you find it." Before Wiggleworth could

36

stop him, the Portal Master leaned forward and ripped a page from the Book of Power. Eon looked sadly at his old friend. "I'm sorry Wiggleworth. I know you don't want any part of the Book to leave the Archive, but a sacrifice must be made. This scrap of paper will glow if it comes into contact with any of the segments of the Mask."

He handed the page to Gill, who tucked it into his belt.

"I understand," Wiggleworth grumbled, "but I insist we transport Gill to Deep Water Wasteland in one of our airships, just in case."

Eon nodded, giving Gill one last smile. "Spyro will stay here with me while I study the rest of the Book, but I will send you help should you require it."

Gill puffed out his chest.

"By swim or fin, Gill Grunt will win!" he said proudly. "I won't let you down, Master."

CHAPTER FOUR

LAST CHANCE COVE

Gill Grunt frowned as the Warrior Librarians' airship touched down at Last Chance Cove, the harbour that nestled on the edge of Deep Water Wasteland. It wasn't that it was a bad landing (quite the opposite in fact – the pilot was almost as skilled as Gill's friend Flynn). Neither was it the fact that Last Chance Cove smelled of pungent puffer-fish and stinky sardines – Gill Grunt was a Gillman. They used fish oil as aftershave.

No, what annoyed Gill was that they'd been forced to moor the airship alongside a dirty great pirate ship – the Fearsome Fang, no less.

Gill hated pirates. He detested pirates. He would be happy if he never saw another pirate again for as long as he lived. The reason was simple: pirates had snatched away the love of his life. Long ago, before he was a Skylander, Gill had joined the Gillmen Marines, a crack force of seawater soldiers. On his first tour of duty, he had been patrolling a misty lagoon when he'd heard a beautiful voice singing an enchanting song. It was a mermaid. In fact, it was the most gorgeous mermaid Gill had ever seen. Within seconds Gill was head-over-flippers in love.

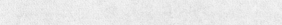

Unfortunately, his platoon still had to combat an army of spit spiders that were marauding along the coast. Gill vowed to return to his love when his tour of duty was over, but when he found his way back to the lagoon, the mermaid was nowhere to be seen.

It was only later that he discovered she had been fin-napped by pirates. Gill searched all over Skylands for his bescaled beloved. Eventually, he met Eon, but even the majestic Portal Master had been unable to track her down. She was lost forever, although Gill still believed in his herring-heart of hearts that he'd find her again one day.

Ever since, the mere whiff of a pirate had made his scales shake with fury. As he stood on the harbour side, glaring at the Fearsome Fang, Gill told himself that he couldn't let himself get distracted – he had a mission to complete. Frowning so hard his eyebrows hurt, Gill shoved through a bunch of Skystone-playing pirates and headed towards the inn that stood on the other side of the port, *The Octopus's Arms.*

As he barged by the pirates, he nudged the arm of a Squiddler. The slimy-faced buccaneer slipped, his deck of cards dropping from his fingers. Roaring with anger, the pirate turned on Gill, shoving a mollusc mortar gun in the Gillman's face. Instinctively, Gill brought his own weapon to bear, pointing his power hose straight in the Squiddler's snarling tentacles. "Great", thought Gill, "just what I didn't want to happen".

As if that wasn't bad enough, Gill was soon surrounded by the Squiddler's crewmates. Without even turning, he could smell the wet doggy stink of the seadogs who were drawing their cutlasses behind him. To his right, a Blastaneer was already hoisting a cannon up to its broad shoulders and to his left a massive Squidface Brute lumbered up, an enormous anchor held threateningly in its hands.

Gill Grunt was completely outnumbered. Even with all his training, he probably wouldn't win this fight. One lone fish against a bunch of barnacle-incrusted, muscle-bound buffoons. The odds were stacked against him and the situation was grim.

It was just as he liked it. A smile spread across Gill's face as he felt his trigger.

WHOOSH!

Behind them a huge tentacle shot out of the sea. Gill gaped as the monstrous arm came crashing down, smashing *The Octopus's Arms* to smithereens. The standoff was forgotten as more

tentacles burst out of the water, grabbing at the onlookers who, quite sensibly, started to scatter. Pirates and landlubbers alike ran for cover as the gigantic tentacles began picking them off one by one. Even the Squidface Brute was plucked from his feet and thrown into the air.

Finally, the head of the monster broke through the water's surface. Gill found himself staring into a pair of milky-white eyes the size of houses.

It was a Cloud Kraken, one of the giant squid-like creatures that lived in the depths of the Deep Sea Wasteland. The monster let out an ear-splitting roar and swallowed the squealing Squidface Brute with one great gulp.

None of this made sense. Despite their size and scary appearance, Cloud Krakens were gentle giants. Kind and docile, they lived in harmony with other sea creatures. Gill had never seen one acting like this.

"Wait!" Gill Grunt shouted up at the sea monster, even as it wrapped three of its awesome

arms around the Warrior Librarian's airship. "There's no need for any of this. Calm down."

It was no good. With another bellow, the Cloud Kraken tightened its tentacles, splitting the ship in two. Warrior Librarians dived to safety as the two halves of the colossal craft sank beneath the waves.

If he couldn't talk the Cloud Kraken down, Gill would have to find another way to stop it. He swung up his water cannon and pointed it straight between the Cloud Kraken's glassy eyes. Even that wasn't right. Cloud Krakens' eyes were usually luminous green, but he'd worry about that later – for now he need to save everyone on the harbour side. Even the Pirates!

Gill was just about to fire when a titanic tentacle slid around his ankle. No! The Cloud Kraken had grabbed him. Gill was lifted off his feet, his water cannon slipping from his webbed fingers. Try as he might, he couldn't free himself from the Cloud Kraken's sticky suckers and could only watch in terror as he was carried towards the monster's snarling mouth.

The Cloud Kraken was going to eat him alive.

CHAPTER FIVE

KRAKEN ATTACK

Gill Grunt struggled as he plunged towards the Cloud Kraken's slavering maw, but the tentacle wouldn't budge. Then, out of the corner of his eye he spotted a flash of light on the harbour side below. It was a Portal! Gill grinned as he saw two newcomers appear out of thin air. It was Zap and Wham-Shell, his fellow Water Skylanders.

"Up here!" he yelled, waving desperately as he dangled in mid-air. Zap looked up, his mouth dropping open.

"What are you doing?" shouted the water dragon.

"Oh, you know, just hanging about," replied

Gill, rolling his eyes. "GET ME DOWN FROM HERE!"

"Alright, keep your fins on," replied Zap, taking a deep breath. Gill closed his eyes, knowing what was coming. A bolt of electricity shot from the dragon's mouth and slammed into the Cloud Kraken's tentacle. Sparks crackled up and down the suckers, sizzling against Gill's own skin. The Cloud Kraken released its grip and Gill tumbled back down to the deck, right into the armoured arms of Wham-Shell.

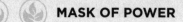

"Th-th-th-th-th-th-hank y-y-y-y-ou," Gill stammered, still juddering from the electric shock. "Y-y-y-you s-s-s-saved m-m-me!"

"I've always said I was a bright spark," Zap grinned showing two rows of razor sharp teeth. "What's that thing?"

"Trouble," replied Wham-Shell, hefting his mighty mace onto his shoulder. "I've never seen a Cloud Kraken acting like this!"

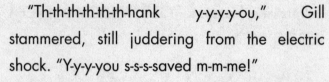

"I – I know," Gill said, his gills still tingling. "It gone mad." Behind them, the monster snatched up pirates and started to toss them from tentacle to tentacle. Zap's mouth dropped.

"Woah! It's juggling them!" the water dragon exclaimed.

"Just when I thought today couldn't get any stranger," Gill said, forcing himself to concentrate on one problem at a time. "OK, there are a lot of Warrior Librarians in the water."

"But they can't swim," pointed out Wham-Shell.

"Exactly. You and Zap rescue them. I'll deal with our colossal circus performer."

The Skylanders didn't need to be told twice. Zap and Wham-Shell were almost at the water's edge as Gill recovered his water cannon. He primed the weapon and let lose a stream of ice-cold water. The gushing torrent hit the creature between the eyes, but it didn't even flinch. As it continued juggling the terrified buccaneers, the sea monster turned its head towards Gill and blasted a thick stream of inky black goo right back towards him. In the sea, the ink was the Cloud Kraken's main defence mechanism. If attacked it would spit it into the water and escape in the middle of the sticky black cloud.

 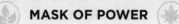
On land, it was just as effective – although the Cloud Kraken showed no desire to escape anywhere. The gunk plastered everything on the dock, Gill Grunt included. Gill tried to stay on his feet, but the stuff was too slippery. He landed with a splat on his back. "Some hero," he thought, wiping the ooze from his eyes.

It was then that the idea struck him. Hardly able to see what he was doing, Gill thrust the barrel of his water cannon into the sea of slime and threw his weapon into reverse. Instead of shooting out water from his water barrel, the gun sucked up the gunge.

When his barrel was full of the goo, Gill once again targeted the Cloud Kraken's face.

"Have some of your own medicine!" he shouted, squeezing the trigger. A column of black, inky gloop sprayed from the cannon, covering the Cloud Kraken's face. The creature howled in surprise, instantly dropping the pirates it had been juggling. Luckily, Zap was already on the case. Sliding on the sea of black slime, the water dragon shot around the harbour, expertly catching each and every plummeting pirate. Gill grinned. His friend sure was fast.

The pirates themselves weren't so happy. They were gasping in horror as the Cloud Kraken, blinded by its own goo, turned on their ship. It was going to destroy the Fearsome Fang.

CHAPTER SIX

CAPTAIN
GRIMSLOBBER

The Cloud Kraken reared out of the water, ready to pull the Fearsome Fang down to the bottom of the ocean. All around Gill, the pirates unsheathed their cutlasses and hefted cannons onto their shoulders, but the Skylander knew they wouldn't even scratch the blinded Cloud Kraken's hide.

On the deck of the Fearsome Fang, the doors of the captain's quarters burst open. The pirate crew gasped as Captain Grimslobber stepped into the sunlight and turned to face the furious sea monster. Why wasn't the Captain running for his life? Couldn't he see that the Fearsome Fang was seconds away from being destroyed?

Then the most curious thing happened. The Captain simply stood, hands on hips and stared at the Cloud Kraken. He didn't shout. He didn't move. He just stared. Even the flock of parrots on his shoulders joined in, glaring at the sea monster for all their worth.

This in itself wasn't all that strange. Captain Grimslobber was famous for being incredibly

brave. Cruel yes, black hearted definitely, but brave all the same. If the Fearsome Fang was about to go down, Captain Grimslobber would go with it. Nothing would get the malevolent mutt to back down, not even a crazed Cloud Kraken.

No, it was the crazed Cloud Kraken itself that was behaving oddly. As soon as Grimslobber appeared on deck, the deranged sea monster froze, mid-attack. One minute the flailing tentacles were waving frantically in the air, the next they were stock-still. The creature looked like a gigantic statue, its milky-white eyes staring balefully down.

Grimslobber thrust out a ring-covered hand, pointing out to sea, and miraculously, unbelievably, the Cloud Kraken turned tail and plunged back beneath the waves, swimming back to the depths.

On the harbour side, the pirates cheered, throwing their hats into the air in celebration. A few of the less safety conscious buccaneers also threw their cutlasses into the air, forgetting that they'd have to catch them again on the way down. With all the Warrior Librarians saved, Zap and Wham-Shell rejoined Gill.

"What happened there?" asked Zap as the

pirate Captain took a bow. "Did the Cloud Kraken just get bored of causing chaos?"

"I've no idea," replied Gill honestly. "I thought Grimslobber was a goner."

"The Cap'n a goner?" chipped in a dog-faced pirate with bones woven into his beard. "Never. The Cap'n be the bravest pirate in all of Skylands!"

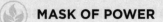

"The stupidest you mean," said Wham-Shell. "Taking on a Cloud Kraken in a staring competition?"

Wham-Shell's comment drew a withering, fish-eyed glare from Gill. Even as much as Gill hated pirates, he knew there would be little benefit to antagonizing so many of them.

"Worked though, didn't it?" Bonebeard pointed out. "He managed to banish the beast. Unlike you lot."

"Pirate Cap'n one, Skylanders nil," added another buccaneer, a Squiddler covered head to tentacle in tattoos of Grimslobber. He must have been the Captain's biggest fan.

"I still thinks the place is cursed," said a third, particularly scrawny pirate. "First there were the crabs and now this."

"Shut yer mouth, ye lily-livered loon," warned Bonebeard. "Remember what the Cap'n said. Loose lips sink schooners, and all that."

Gill was intrigued. "What crabs?"

"Chased ol' Gut-Rot off the ship, they did," the tattooed pirate said and was rewarded with a clout around the head from Bonebeard. "Oww!"

Behind Gill, Wham-Shell stifled a snigger at the thought of a chef being given his just desert by marauding crabs.

"Then there was that eel I found tying itself in knots on the dock," added the scrawny pirate. "Ain't that right, Squid-Ink?"

"Yer not wrong, Runtface," agreed the tattooed pirate, rubbing his sore head. "And don't forget the starfish you were going to eat for yer supper last night."

"As if I could," said Runtface sadly. "Jumped right off me plate and did a tap dance up and down the bar."

"It did what?" Gill asked. Now he'd heard everything.

"What did I tell yer?" Runtface fixed the Gillman with a doom-laden glare. "The place is cursed, I tells yer. Cursed."

"What's all this nonsense, I hears." The voice boomed over the harbour, deep and gruff. The throng of pirates parted to reveal Captain Grimslobber striding towards the Skylanders on his two wooden legs. "Runtface, ye flea-bitten swab, is I going to have to keelhaul ye again? Or does ye want to walk the plank?"

"N-no, Cap'n," Runtface stammered, quaking in his boots, "Sorry Cap'n. I was just saying, Cap'n –"

"I knows what ye were saying," growled Grimslobber as he came to a halt in front of Gill. "Utter nonsense, the lot of it. I told yer before, there be no curse." His cruel eyes rested upon Gill and he grinned a golden grin. "Now, what do we have here? I thought I smelt something fishy."

Beside Gill, Wham-Shell slapped his Malacostracan Mace into an armoured palm. "I'd show some respect if I were you."

"Wham-Shell's right dude," Zap agreed,

electricity arcing across his gold harness in warning. "That was a shocking thing to say."

Gill raced a webbed hand to calm his friends. Grimslobber was just trying to pick a fight. They all needed to keep their tempers in check and remember why they were here.

"The Captain's just having a little joke," the Gillman said, his eyes falling on the satchel Grimslobber was wearing across his impressive chest. Gill could see that there was something bulky tucked inside, wrapped in a dirty, old rag. A strange thing for a seadog so concerned about his appearance to carry. "He meant no harm."

"No harm at all," jeered Grimslobber, tucking the satchel behind his back. Had he spotted Gill looking at it? "I'm sorry if my crew have been boring you with their shaggy dog stories. They lets their imaginations run away sometimes."

"Must have been all the excitement with the Cloud Kraken," said Gill, not believing a word of it.

"Aye, that it be," nodded Grimslobber, the sunlight glinting off his jewelry. "Strange things happen at sea."

"And getting stranger by the minute," added Squid-Ink, causing Bonebeard to roll his eyes in dismay. "Perhaps we should give up diving for treasure until –"

The tattooed pirate didn't finish the sentence. He was too busy recovering from another clout around the lugholes from Bonebeard. "You heard the Cap'n, you scurvy sop," the dog-faced pirate growled. "Shut yer cake hole."

But it was too late. The cat was well and truly out of the bag.

"Treasure?" asked Zap, "What treasure is that?"

Gill groaned. The water dragon was always too curious for his own good. Zap had a nose for trouble. Well, a snout at least.

Grimslobber's smile faded and, quick as a flash, he'd drawn both of his cutlasses. "None of yer business, Skylander."

The other pirates didn't need prompting. Within seconds every sword, knife and cannon on the quayside was pointing at the three Skylanders.

"Now, lets not be so hasty," said Gill, priming his water cannon just in case. "We don't want any trouble. Just let us go and we'll let you get back to your treasure, no questions asked."

The pirates paused, considered this for a second, and then attacked anyway.

CHAPTER SEVEN

PIRATE FIGHT

The Skylanders were outnumbered four to one. With a deafening cheer, the pirates charged, cutlasses ready to chop and cannons ready to fire. The first shot came from Squid-Ink who let loose with his Mollusc Mortar Gun, blasting a barrage of blowfish straight at the Skylanders. Luckily Wham-Shell was ready for action. Swinging his massive mace like a bat, he whacked the exploding fish back towards the pirates. Squid-Ink's googly eyes grew even wider as a blowfish hit him wetly in the chest and detonated, sending him barrelling backwards into his fellow buccaneers.

It was exactly the distraction the Skylanders needed. Catching Zap's eye, Gill spun on his webbed feet, firing his water cannon in an arc, soaking every pirate in turn. Then it was Zap's turn. The water dragon opened his mouth and spat out a bolt of crackling electricity. Long ago, Zap had been raised by a family of electric eels, and the first lesson his adopted mother had taught him was that water and electricity don't

mix. Zap's electricity sparked and fizzed as it jumped from one sodden pirate to another. The pirates shook and stammered, yellow sparks dancing along cutlass blades, golden teeth chattering in tentacled mouths and electrified dog hair standing on end.

"Quick!" Gill yelled, darting through a gap in the wall of shocked scallywags. "Make for the water."

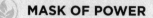

Grimslobber lunged at Wham-Shell as the crustacean charged past, his cutlasses narrowly missing the Skylander's crusty shell. As he dashed after his friends, Zap managed to deliver an extra static charge to the pirate Captain's gold belt. Grimslobber yelped as his trousers fell down around his ankles, revealing a pair of skull-and-crossbones underpants. The Captain stumbled and landed face first in a sizzling puddle of Zap's sea slime. "That's what you get for calling Gill names," Zap shouted over his shoulder, before plunging beneath the waves.

On the quayside, Grimslobber pushed himself up and shook a fist after the Skylanders. "You'll walk me plank for this, ye scurvy wretches,"

he snarled as his flock of slightly singed parrots settled back on his broad shoulders. "Grimslobber shall 'ave 'is revenge!"

Some distance from the dock, Gill's head broke the surface. He could see the pirate crew gathering their dropped weapons, still shaking from the effects of Zap's charge. Beside him, the water dragon and Wham-Shell popped up from beneath the waves, just in time to see a Portal appear in mid-air. Spyro flew out of the ball of bright light, his wings flapping to keep him hovering above the water.

"Gill, are you OK?" Spyro asked, looking down at his friend. "Master Eon said you were having pirate problems."

"Yeah, they were pretty re-volt-ing," joked Zap.

"But we soon had them shell-shocked," rumbled Wham-Shell.

"The Warrior Librarians are in a pretty bad way though," pointed out Gill. "Their armour is

 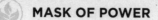
completely water-logged."

"Already taken care of," Spyro said, nodding at the quayside.

On the dock, lights flared. Eon was transporting the survivors of the shipwreck back to the Eternal Archive.

"So what next?" Zap asked. "We still have no idea where the Mask segment is."

"No," agreed Gill, "but I know someone who may be able to help. Fancy a little dip Spyro?"

"I'll stick to the skies thanks," the purple dragon said. "But you better get going – look."

Gill followed Spyro's gaze. A single, solitary cloud had appeared on the horizon. A particularly evil looking cloud.

"Kaos!" Zap snarled. "But how did that little twerp know to look for the segment here?"

"That's what we're trying to find out," Spyro said, another Portal appearing beside him. "We can't let Kaos find the fragment first."

Gill flashed Spyro a swift salute. "We're on

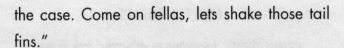
the case. Come on fellas, lets shake those tail fins."

"But where are we going?" Wham-Shell asked, still none the wiser.

"To visit an old friend," Gill said, before plunging beneath the waves. Wham-Shell shrugged and followed suit, while Zap leapt out of the water, pulled off a perfect triple somersault and dived below the surface.

"Catch you later, dude!" the water dragon yelled before disappearing.

Left on his own, Spyro looked from the approaching cloud to the pirate ship on the dock.

"I just hope no one catches you, Zap," he muttered to himself, flying back into the Portal.

CHAPTER EIGHT

THE KINGDOM OF THE MERPEOPLE

It felt good to be back in the water. It had been ages since Gill had enjoyed a deep-sea dive. At first, he'd been worried that they'd run into the Cloud Kraken again, but the murderous sea monster was nowhere to be seen. That still troubled him. What had turned such a meek creature into a raging beast? He'd never seen anything like it. Was it linked somehow to the segment of the Mask? It seemed too much of a coincidence if it wasn't.

Zap swept down beside Gill, air-bubbles

streaming from the canisters he wore on his back. Gill smiled. If you thought Zap was speedy on land, seeing him underwater was something else. He swam like greased lightning.

"So," Zap asked, talking bubble-language, the only way to speak beneath the waves, "where are we heading?"

"You'll see," Gill replied, leading them through a deep gully in the seabed. Moving as one, the three Skylanders shot over a family of waving anemones and raced towards a cliff.

They were almost there. Beyond the cliff, Gill could already make out a soft glow and felt a tingle of anticipation flicker over his fins. He was so excited he had tadpoles in his stomach.

Gill was pleased to see Zap's mouth drop as soon as they cleared the cliff. For once the fast-talking dragon was lost for words. Gill couldn't blame him. Below them, a majestic palace rose up from the seabed, luminescent coral towers stretching as far as the eye could see. A flag bearing a regal coat of arms flapped from the tallest turret – a shell-encrusted shield flanked by two imposing sea horses.

"Woah, what is this place?" whispered a wide-eyed Zap.

"The Kingdom of the Merpeople," Gill replied proudly. "The oldest underwater race in all of Skylands – and my friends. If anyone knows the location of the segment it'll be them. They've swam these waters for thousands of years."

They swam on in silence, sweeping down

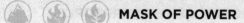

seaweed-lined avenues towards a pair of huge barnacled gates. It was as beautiful as Gill remembered, but something didn't seem right. Guards should have appeared above the gates by now, ready to ask them their business – but there was no one there.

"Is no one home?" asked Zap as they reached the gates.

Wham-Shell swam forward and rapped three times on the heavy doors. The sound reverberated through the water until a head finally popped over the gatehouse's rampart.

78

"Who goes there?" the solitary guard asked.

Gill swam up so he could be seen.

"It's me, Gill Grunt."

"What do you want?"

Gill's frown deepened. Usually his name was enough to open the gates.

"Erm, I'm here to see King Scalebeard, ruler of this kingdom."

"Whatever you're selling, we're not interested. Sling your hook!"

Zap floated up to join the Gillman.

"Thought you were friends with these dudes?"

"So did I," Gill admitted, utterly confused. He turned back to the guard. "You don't understand. We're here on Skylander business."

"Oh, Skylander business," the guard said. "That makes all the difference."

"It does?" Gill said hopefully.

"No," replied the guard. "Not in the slightest. Now stop carping on and push off."

And with that the guard disappeared back

over the ramparts.

"I don't believe it," said Gill, his heart sinking. "I've never been denied entrance before."

"Hey, chill out." Zap gave Gill a friendly nudge in the wetsuit. "We're underwater. We can just swim over the battlements."

"No we can't," Gill explained, "The Kingdom is defended by a magic shield. The only way in is through the gates."

"Then I suggest we knock a little louder," Wham-Shell shouted from below. Gill looked down. The crustacean was whirling his mace around and around, picking up speed as he prepared to let it go. The Gillman gaped as he realized what Wham-Shell was planning to do. As the son of an underwater king himself, the pumped-up crab wasn't used to being refused anything. By now both Wham-Shell and the mace were nothing more than a red blur, spinning so fast that the water churned around them. Then, with a grunt of effort, Wham-Shell let go of its handle and the mace shot towards the gates. With an ear-splitting crunch, the gates were ripped from their hinges and sent spiraling back into the castle's courtyard.

"Now they'll let us in," boomed Wham-Shell as his mace returned magically to his open hand.

"It might not be that easy," advised Gill, slotting a quadent harpoon into his water cannon. This wasn't how he'd imagined events unfolding. "King Scalebeard's guards will already be rushing to stop us."

Zap didn't look convinced, although he'd charged up his golden harness just in case.

"Unless they're really small, I don't see anyone rushing anywhere. Any chance the King's guards are the size of plankton?"

Zap was right. The courtyard beyond the gatehouse looked absolutely deserted. No guards. No merpeople. No anyone.

"Let's go," yelled Zap, streaking forward,

electricity crackling in his wake. Gill watched Wham-Shell follow the dragon in confusion. Where was everyone? Clutching his water cannon, Gill slipped through the gates. Usually thousands of mer-knights would have been charging towards them by now, brandishing super-sharp swords and spears. Instead, all that greeted them was a startled school of minnows that scattered as he swam by.

"Ow!"

A shell bounced off Gill's head. He turned to see the lone guard throwing shells after them. Gill raised his cannon, but let it drop immediately. The guard was no more than a mer-child, dressed in armour that was far too large for him.

As Gill swam out of range, he felt a chill spread through his guts. Why were children defending the city's walls? Something was very wrong here.

CHAPTER NINE

KING SCALEBEARD

The streets of the kingdom were as deserted as the main courtyard. The three Skylanders swam passed overturned market stalls, abandoned houses and overgrown seaweed on their way to the palace. Usually the royal gardens were pristine, Gill thought, before correcting himself – usually the royal gardens were crowded.

Finally, they spotted someone, an elderly merman snoozing on a hammock slung between two coral lampposts.

"Wakey wakey," called Zap, but the old-timer

did not stir. He just kept on slumbering, gulping in mouthfuls of water with each snore. Even a short, sharp shock from Zap's electric breath didn't wake the guy. He just muttered something and then rolled over in his hammock.

"What did he say?" asked Wham-Shell.

"I think he asked why I couldn't leave him alone like everyone else . . ."

"Who else?" asked Gill. "There's no one here."

"You said it," said Zap. "I've no idea why you thought coming here would help us find the fragment. The place is a ghost town."

"At least someone's at home," said Wham-Shell, pointing up at the tower that loomed over them. "Unless they left a light on."

Gill looked up. Sure enough, a solitary light was burning in a stained glass window high above.

"That's the throne room," Gill said excitedly. "King Scalebeard must still be here." He hurried towards the tower's door. "Come on. He'll be able to tell us what's been happening."

"I've no idea what's been happening!" said King Scalebeard. The King looked even older and frailer than the last time Gill had seen him. His white beard, once bushy and full, was all scraggly, and his eyes were sunken and red-rimmed. It looked like the King hadn't slept in weeks. His children looked no better. Prince Aquan, the next in line to the throne, sat to the King's right, while the beautiful Princess Finella sat to his left. Both looked as worried as their father.

At least here in the throne room there were some mer-knights, although Gill had expected at least three dozen rather than just, well, three.

"But where is everyone?" Gill asked. The King frowned and lifted a giant, twisty shell to his ear. Scalebeard was slightly hard of hearing.

"Beg pardon?" the King asked.

"I said, where is everyone?" Gill shouted into the ear trumpet.

"Eh?"

"WHERE IS EVERYONE?" Gill bellowed.

"OK, OK, there's no need to shout," the cloth-eared King complained. "I wish I knew. I turned my back for a second and half the kingdom swam away."

"Where have they gone?" asked Zap.

"Say again sonny?"

"Where. Have. They. Gone?" the sea dragon repeated, through gritted teeth.

"You'd like to sing a song? What's the young fellow talking about?"

"No one knows," interrupted Prince Aquan, prompting another puzzled look from his father. "It began about three weeks ago. Our subjects just started swimming away."

"They dropped everything they were doing," continued Princess Finella. "Mermen, mermaids, even little mergirls and merboys."

"Only the eldest and the infirm were left behind," Aquan said. "There's hardly anyone left."

"But surely you sent soldiers to see where they were going?" asked Wham-Shell.

"Of course," replied Finella. "But they never came back either."

"It's like their minds have been . . ." Aquan's words trailed off.

"Like their minds have been what, your majesty?" Gill prompted, but the Prince didn't reply. He was just staring past them, into the distance.

"What are you young people chattering about," asked King Scalebeard, shaking his ear trumpet in frustration. "I can't hear a thing."

"Neither can they," Zap said waving a hand in front of Aquan's eyes. The Prince didn't flinch.

"They're in some kind of trance."

Finella was the same, as were the three mer-knights. Worst of all, their eyes were beginning to turn glassy and milky-white.

"Just like the Cloud Kraken," Gill exclaimed.

"What is going on?" demanded the King, even as his knights dropped their spears and began to swim silently towards the throne-room's stained glass windows. "Aquan, Finella? Where are you going? Oh no, not you as well."

Sure enough, the Prince and Princess were following the knights, their faces slack, their eyes white as chalk.

Gill tried to grab Finella's hand, to hold her back. The Princess's head snapped around, her pretty mouth twisting into a snarl. She swiped at Gill with her long tail, thwacking him across the chest and sending him spinning back into Wham-Shell. Then she turned back to the window and continued on her way.

Zap shot forward, putting himself between the window and the entranced merfolk.

"Oh no you don't," he cried defiantly, only to be grabbed by the horns by the first knight and tossed out of the way like a soggy-rag doll.

"OK, maybe you do," he yelped as he crashed into a suit of armour.

Picking up speed, the lead knight swam straight through the window, followed by the others. Gill made one last grab for the Princess's tail but they were gone, swimming up into the ocean.

"I thought the Kingdom was protected by a magical shield," said Zap.

"That's just to stop people getting in," Gill swam up to the smashed window and peered outside. "Not to stop people getting out."

All across the city, the remaining merfolk were

abandoning their homes, streaming up to who knew where, each as glassy-eyed as the next.

"We have to get after them!" Wham-Shell had joined the others by the window, his fingers flexing around his mace's shaft. "Find out where they're heading."

Gill swam back to the glum-looking King.

"What's the point of a King with no one to rule?" the old man was muttering, "I might as well retire and grow anemones. At least anemones don't leave you."

"Don't worry, your majesty," Gill said, trying to sound calmer than he felt. "We'll find out where they're going. We'll get them back."

"Eh?" the King said, thrusting the ear trumpet to his ear. "You fancy a snack? How can you think of food at a time like this?"

"Never mind," Gill said, swimming back to the window. "Come on you two. Follow those merpeople!"

King Scalebeard sat back on his throne and

watched the Skylanders slip through the broken window.

"I don't know," he said to himself, looking around the empty throne room in dismay. "Young people today. They never listen."

"They . . . sure . . . swim . . . fast," puffed Wham-Shell, struggling to keep up thanks to his heavy armour.

"Not fast enough." Zap shot by in a blaze of crackling electricity, hot on the heels, or at least the fins, of the fleeing merfolk. "Grab on."

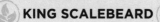
Catching Zap's drift, Gill snatched hold of Zap's short, stubby tail with one hand and Wham-Shell's claws with the other. They rocketed forward and had soon caught up with the shoal of zombified merpeople.

"Hey!" shouted Gill, as they sped through the glassy-eyed throng. "Wake up! You all need to wake up." He let go of Zap and swam towards a bulky merman with a bushy green beard. "What's happened to you? Where are you going?"

"I think I can answer that," gulped Wham-Shell, pointing ahead. Gill looked and moaned softly. Just when he thought today couldn't get any worse.

"Is that what I think it is, dude?" asked Zap.

Gill nodded. "I'm afraid so. Electro-jellies."

Of all the many creatures that live in Deep Water Wasteland, electro-jellies are the worst. They look like normal jellyfish – if normal jellyfish are the size of elephants and pack a 10,000-volt punch, that is. Brush against just one of an electro-jelly's many dainty-looking fronds and you'll receive a jolt that makes Zap's own electric breath feel like a feather-light tickle.

Oh, there's another major difference. Normal jellyfish just hang around in the water, minding their own business until someone blunders into their tentacles. Electro-jellies are more pro-active.

"They've spotted us!" boomed Wham-Shell. "Watch out!"

If any of the entranced merpeople heard the crabby prince they didn't respond. They carried on swimming towards the brood of electro-jellies, even as the devilish creatures started pushing towards them, fronds flailing out in greeting.

"Stop them!" shouted Gill, trying to grab the green-bearded merman. "They'll never make it."

"Try telling them that!" replied Wham-Shell, grappling with a mer-knight, only to find the soldier's gauntleted hands grabbing his own armour plating. "Hang on. Aren't we supposed to be grabbing them?"

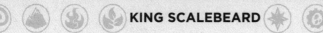

Gill didn't answer. He was too busy trying to remove himself from the clutches of greenbeard. The merman had clamped a burly arm around Gill's neck. The merpeople were pulling the Skylanders into the oncoming electro-jellies!

Gill thrashed as hard as he could, but couldn't get the merman's arm to budge. He glanced up to see a mass of sparkling fronds rushing towards him. He squeezed his eyes shut and waited for the first electric shock. This wasn't going to be pleasant.

CHAPTER TEN

THE GUPPY GATES

The shock never came. Even with his eyes squeezed shut, Gill could feel himself being twisted back and forth. He opened one eye and wished that he hadn't. All he could see was a throng of fluffy pink fronds – fluffy pink fronds sparking with 10,000 volts apiece.

But, amazingly, every time a tentacle drifted dangerously close, the green-bearded merman changed direction, dodging left and right to avoid being stung. Gill twisted in the merman's grip to look at his captor's face. The eyes were still white and glassy, but somehow the entranced

97

merman was keeping Gill safe.

The water sparked beside Gill's right ear as a tentacle breezed a little too close and then they were through, shooting clear of the attacking brood. As Gill watched, the mer-knight dragging Wham-Shell appeared from the mass of electro-jellies, the eyes beneath his helmet staring blankly ahead.

The merpeople had saved them! They may have been mindlessly swimming to Eon-knew where, but they'd still got them through without a scratch. These were the merpeople he knew and loved, not these glassy-eyed zombies.

Gill turned to say thanks, but didn't have a chance. Green-beard suddenly relaxed his grip and powered on, leaving an increasingly bewildered Gill Grunt floating away. Wham-Shell had also been released and swam up to join his friend.

"That's no way to travel, if you ask me," the royal crab said, "although I bet Zap enjoyed it!"

"Zap!" Gill exclaimed. "Where is he?"

The two of them looked around, but the water dragon was nowhere to be seen. Perhaps he hadn't been so lucky? Perhaps he had got stung? Even though Zap could manipulate electricity himself, there was no telling if his energy harness could absorb that much power. Gill peered down to the mass of electro-jellies below. "He must still be in there."

Wham-Shell sighed. "I've got a horrible feeling I know what you're going to say next."

"We've got to go back in."

"Yup, that's the one. I've got a horrible feeling you mean it too."

"Of course I do." Gill didn't wait around to argue. They couldn't leave Zap injured and alone in a sea of electro-jellies. They had to rescue him.

Bracing themselves, Gill and Wham-Shell swam back towards the electro-jellies, only to see a flash of blue in the midst of all the deadly pink

jelly. Like a cork flying from a bottle, Zap shot from the middle of the school of electro-jellies, an unconscious merman held fast in his jaws.

"Zap, you made it!" Gill exclaimed happily.

"Course I did, dude." Zap came to a halt beside them, opening his mouth to release the sparked-out merman. "That was rad. We've gotta do it again."

Gill wasn't so sure about that. "Hopping halibut, that's Prince Aquan."

"His mer-majesty got zapped by one of the electro-jellies," Zap explained, still buzzing from his wild ride through the deadly sea-creatures.

"Knocked him out. I only just got him out before he became a jelly snack."

The Prince groaned, coming round. Sleepily he opened his eyes.

"Look," said Gill. "His eyes are normal. They're not glassy at all!"

"G-Gill," Aquan stammered. "What happened?"

"That's what we hoped you could tell us," admitted Wham-Shell. "Why did you leave the palace?"

Aquan looked confused, his regal brow creasing as he tried to remember. "The voice told us to come."

"What voice?" Gill asked, the memory of the black cloud on the horizon springing to mind. Was this all Kaos' doing?

"I don't know," replied the Prince sadly. "The last thing I remember was being in the throne-room with my sister and . . ." He trailed off. "Finella. Where's Finella?"

Without another word, Aquan powered after

the rest of the merpeople, desperate to find his zombified-sister.

"Here we go again," grumbled Wham-Shell as he began to swim after the Prince. Giggling, Zap grabbed the crustacean's carapace and shot forward. "Come on slow poke. I'll give you a lift."

The Prince had found his sister by the time the Skylanders had caught up. He was shaking Finella gently by the shoulders, trying to rouse her from her milky-eyed trance.

"Come on Finella. It's me, Aquan."

"It's no good, your majesty," Gill said, swimming up beside them. "We tried, but we couldn't break the spell. The magic that is controlling them is too strong."

"But I must stop them," Aquan argued, his face lined with worry. "I just must . . . I must . . ."

A strange look passed over the Prince's features, as if he was fighting something. Gill

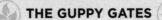

grabbed Aquan's arm.

"Your majesty, what's wrong?"

"I must . . ." Aquan's face went slack and he closed his eyes, his voice dreamlike, free of any emotion. "I must . . . follow the voice."

When Aquan opened his eyes again, they were glassy and milky-white.

"He's been taken over again," said Zap, as the Prince's arm slipped out of Gill's grasp. "Totally bogus!"

"Must follow," the Prince droned as he rejoined his sister and the rest of the hypnotized merpeople. "Must follow."

"Let me guess," murmured Wham-Shell, "we're going to do a bit more following ourselves."

This time they didn't have to swim far. The entranced merpeople were heading towards a long rubber pipe that snaked down from the surface.

"What's that thing?" asked Zap as the

merpeople swam down to the seabed.

"No idea," admitted Gill, "Maybe some kind of air line."

"Whatever it is, it's burrowed straight into the seabed," pointed out Wham-Shell. "See, right by those gates."

Wham-Shell was right. The tube plunged into the rock beside a pair of huge, silver gates that were set into the seabed itself.

"Hang on a minute," Gill said, peering down into the depths. "They're not gates."

"Then what are they?"

"Tiny silver fish, swimming together to form a barrier."

"A barrier to what?" asked Zap, but again Gill had no answer. As the Skylanders watched in amazement, the shoal of fish split in two, parting so the zombified merpeople could swim through.

"Quick!" shouted Gill. "We need to get through those guppy gates before they close."

They swam forward as fast as they could, but it was no good. As the last merman crossed the threshold, the fish swarmed back together, forming the barrier once again. Gill couldn't stop himself. Carried on by his own momentum, he crashed straight into the guppy gates. It was like trying to burst through a trampoline. He bounced off the mass of silvery scales, straight into Wham-Shell.

Zap managed to pull up before he too whacked into the gates. He looked more closely at the tiny fish. "Hey," he called back to his friends. "These little dudes' eyes are glassy and white. Sound familiar?"

"They must be under the thrall of the mysterious voice too," Gill said, swimming nearer. Zap was right. They were all slack-faced, completely under the voice's spell. He pushed against them with both hands. It was no good. They were now packed together so tightly it was like trying to shove your way through a brick wall. Someone

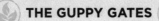
definitely didn't want the Skylanders to get past. If only there was a way to break the spell.

"Of course," Gill slapped his hand against his forehead. Why hadn't he thought of this before? "Aquan broke free of the trance when he was shocked by the electro-jellies. If we could somehow give these fish a little tingle of electricity . . ." He looked at Zap expectantly.

"What about one of my megavolt lightning bolts?" the water dragon asked excitedly, before his face fell. "Oh, hang on. I can't direct my lightning when I'm underwater. You'll get shocked too."

"What if you get really close to the gates," asked Wham-Shell. "If we stand well back . . ."

Zap nodded furiously. "It might work. Yeah, let's give it a go."

While Gill and Wham-Shell swam back to a safe distance, Zap pushed his nose right up to the guppy-gates. "Are you clear?" he shouted back to Gill. "I'm amped and ready to go!"

Gill gave Zap a thumbs up. "Get zapping," he called out, ready to thrust himself forward as soon as the barrier was broken. He watched Zap take a deep breath, preparing to let loose the lightning, when . . .

WHOOSH!

Something zipped past Gill's ear and thudded into Zap.

WHIZZ!

There was another one. Zap cried out as he was hit on the head with a . . . wait, that wasn't possible. It was one of Wham-Shell's starfish bullets.

Gill glanced over his shoulder and gaped at what he saw. Wham-Shell was firing starfish from the end of his enchanted mace. Firing at Zap! But that wasn't the worst of it. His eyes were milky-white.

Gill grappled with his entranced friend, trying to wrestle away the mace, but Wham-Shell swatted him aside as if he was a shrimp.

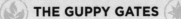

Gill called for Zap to help, but the water dragon needed assistance himself. Stunned by the starfish, Zap was dazed, not even sure which way was up or down.

"Wham-Shell," Gill shouted. "This is wrong. Zap is your friend."

When Wham-Shell replied, the voice was not his own. "Turn back if ye want the water dragon to live."

"What?" Gill spluttered. "You don't mean that, Wham-Shell. This isn't you!"

But Wham-Shell wasn't listening. He was swimming forward to grab the barely conscious Zap. Gill tried to stop him, but had to dive to the side to avoid a bombardment of deadly starfish from Wham-Shell's mace. When he looked up, the gates had opened and Wham-Shell was dragging Zap into the cave beyond.

"Remember, stay away, ye scurvy wretch," Wham-Shell bellowed, before the guppy gates slammed shut behind them.

CHAPTER ELEVEN

THE MINE UNDER THE SEA

Gill didn't know what to do. He knew he had to get past the gates, but he couldn't shock the fish like Zap. How could he break the spell?

"Hang on a minnowing minute," Gill said to himself. "I may not be able to shock the guppies, but I sure can surprise them!"

Gill raised his water cannon, pointing it towards the barrier. He knew blasting it wouldn't do any good, but his trusty weapon could still help. With the flick of a switch, he slammed the cannon in reverse, sucking water into his water barrel. That wasn't all the cannon sucked in. The gates buckled as the fish were pulled into the gun, unable to swim against the current. With a long sucking slurp, they disappeared into the cannon and burst out of the top of the water barrel on Gill's back.

A dizzy guppy swam past, its eyes rolling. Its normal looking eyes. Yes! The fish had been so shocked by their impromptu journey through the cannon's mechanism that the spell had been broken.

Now, for stage two of the plan.

As the gates buckled under the pull of his cannon, Gill flicked the switch again and the weapon fired out a barrage of completed bewildered fish. The dazed tiddlers slapped against their guppies-in-arms and, in the confusion, the barrier broke up, shocked fish scattering everywhere in surprise.

Gill took his chance. Before the gates could reform, he swam as fast as he could, rushing past the mass of flustered fish into the cave.

He was through!

As the gate closed behind him, Gill swam down a dark, rocky tunnel heading towards a soft glow ahead.

What he saw at the end of the channel made his jaw drop. In a massive cave, lit by balls of glowing krill, hundreds of hypnotised merpeople toiled. They were tapping at the walls with rusty pick-axes, digging gem-eels from the rocks. Gill had heard about gem-eels but never seen one. These beautiful jewel-encrusted creatures were made up of thousands of brightly coloured gems. Safe while under the water, the eels simply collapsed into heaps of precious gems when on dry land. Everywhere Gill looked, the entranced merfolk were herding the helpless eels into cages ready to be winched up to the surface. He had to stop them, but first needed to find Wham-Shell and Zap.

Gill nearly jumped out of his scales as he felt hands suddenly slapping down on his shoulders. Twisting around, he found himself staring into the milky-white eyes of Aquan and Finella.

"Ye will come with us," they droned in the same spooky voice Wham-Shell had used.

"No, you don't understand." Gill tried to wrestle free from their grip, but they were too strong. The spell must have been giving them super-strength. As he wriggled, the Prince and Princess dragged him across the cavern towards a massive metal dome that was connected to the pipe they had seen above the seabed. It was a diving bell. Gill hadn't seen one of those for years. Long ago, Mabu used them to explore the many seas of Skylands. They would sit inside the chamber and be lowered beneath the waves, air being pumped down from above.

"Finella, who's inside the bell?" The princess didn't even acknowledge the question, so Gill tried her brother. "Aquan! Listen to me. What's going on?"

"They can't hear ye," came a voice from within the diving bell. "They be completely under me power."

"Captain Grimslobber," Gill hissed as he was brought level to a window in the corroded metal

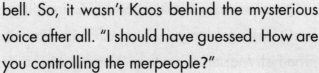
bell. So, it wasn't Kaos behind the mysterious voice after all. "I should have guessed. How are you controlling the merpeople?"

The Captain grinned, removing his pirate hat with a flourish. Underneath he was wearing a tiara made of tiny glittering shells. If the situation wasn't so grim, Gill would have laughed. The Captain looked ridiculous.

"It's all down to this little beauty," Grimslobber said, looking pleased as punch with himself. "The Fish Master's Crown gives me control over any creature of the sea, and I is not just talking about merfolk."

Beside the diving bell, Wham-Shell stepped forward, mace in hand. His eyes were still chalky-white.

"But if you can control sea creatures, why don't you just command the gem-eels to swim into your traps? I assume you're after their jewels."

"Those jewels will make me rich beyond me wildest dreams – and me dreams are pretty wild, I can tell ya," gloated the Captain. "Unfortunately, the gem-eels seem immune to me crown's charms."

"So, you needed the merpeople to dig them out."

The Captain's smirk drew wider still, the parrots on his shoulders flapping around in a frenzy.

"Not just merpeople, Skylander," he sneered. "I don't mind the odd Gillman lending a hand . . ."

"You're joking," Gill scoffed. "I'd never help the likes of . . ."

Gill tried to finish the sentence but his jaw wouldn't move. In fact, nothing would move. His arms were frozen by his sides and, even as he tried to struggle away from the Prince and Princess, his legs wouldn't budge. He couldn't even move his eyes. He was just staring straight ahead. Straight at the Captain.

Straight at his master.

Gill Grunt was under Grimslobber's spell!

CHAPTER **TWELVE**

UNDER THE SPELL

There was nothing Gill could do. No matter how much he tried to fight the spell, he had to do what the Captain commanded. Helplessly he joined the merpeople, digging out the eels and shooing them into the cage. He had no control over his actions, no control at all.

As the first cage was hauled off by an army of hypnotized mermen, Gill tried to grind his teeth in anger, but couldn't even do that unless Grimslobber told him to. He had to find a way of breaking the curse, but how?

As the cage was lifted, a figure was revealed

spread-eagled under a blanket of suffocating starfish. It was Zap, pinned down and unable to move.

"Oh no, not you as well, dude?" Zap moaned when he spotted Gill's milky eyes. "Old Grimface can't control me, because I wasn't born beneath the sea, but I'd hoped you'd be able to escape."

"So did I," Gill thought as he was forced to pick up another pickaxe. Stiffly, the Gillman turned and stalked away from Zap. "But what can I do?"

 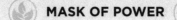

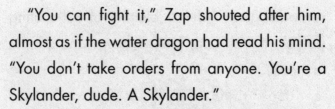

"You can fight it," Zap shouted after him, almost as if the water dragon had read his mind. "You don't take orders from anyone. You're a Skylander, dude. A Skylander."

It was no good. The Fish Master's Crown was too strong. Resistance was impossible. Back at the cave wall, Gill raised the pickaxe high above his head and began to dig.

Zap wasn't giving up. "Just think why we're down here Gill. Remember our mission. We need to find the Water fragment before Kaos. We need to stop him rebuilding the Mask of Power. Eon is relying on you."

The pickaxe stopped swinging for just a second. Zap was right. He'd promised Eon that he wouldn't let him down. By swim or fin, Gill Grunt would win. The pickaxe continued on its way, cracking into the hard rock.

"You told Master Eon you could handle it too," Zap continued, his voice muffled under all those starfish. "He believes in you. So does

Spyro. So do I."

Gill could hardly hear Zap speaking under the TOK, TOK, TOK of the pickaxe, but he could feel anger rising in his chest. Eon and Spyro were relying on him. He couldn't let them down.

"You're Gill Grunt, dude!" Zap shouted almost out of breath. "Remember that! You never give in. You didn't give in at Last Chance Cove, you didn't give in at the guppy gate. You didn't even give in when those pirates kidnapped your girlfriend. You searched all over Skylands for her. You still look for her even now. And you know what dude? You'll find her. You'll find her as surely as you'll beat this curse."

A thousand-and-one faces raced through Gill's hypnotized mind. Eon, Spyro, the love he'd lost all those years ago. He thought of Zap caught beneath the starfish, of Grimslobber laughing to himself within his diving bell – of Kaos rebuilding the Mask. He saw Wham-Shell, under the captain's thrall, Finella, Aquan. They

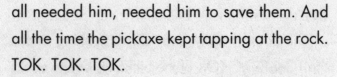

all needed him, needed him to save them. And all the time the pickaxe kept tapping at the rock. TOK. TOK. TOK.

He wouldn't let them down. The merpeople had saved them, even though they were under Grimslobber's spell. They had guided the Skylanders through the electro-jellies. If they could do it, so could he. He was Gill Grunt. He was a Skylander.

The pickaxe stopped mid-swing. With a cry of determination, Gill tossed the tool away. It bounced off the cave-wall and clattered to the floor. Behind him, he heard Zap cheer. He had done it. He had beaten the curse. He was free.

"No!" screamed Grimslobber from within his diving bell. "Ye must obey me. Ye must obey the Fish Master!"

"I don't think so," Gill yelled back. He could feel the crown trying to reassert its control over him, but struggled forward. Each step was an effort, like wading through treacle, but he

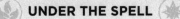
wouldn't let himself be taken over again. Not when his friends needed him. "This ends here, Grimslobber," he hissed through clenched teeth.

Grimslobber was on his feet now, his parrots squawking and flapping around the cramped diving bell. The Captain was pressing the band of shells down on his head, trying to amplify its power, but it was no good.

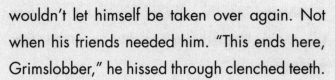

"Gill," Zap cried out excitedly. "Grim-chops is losing control. Look at the merpeople."

All around, the merfolk were swaying, clutching their heads. Their eyes flickered from milky-white to normal and back again. The more Gill battled on, the more difficult it was for the Captain to concentrate. Everyone was fighting back. And they were winning

"Wham-Shell!" the panicking pirate screamed. "Protect yer Fish Master. Batter that flamin' fish!"

A look of confusion on his crab-like features, Wham-Shell lurched forward. He started to swing his mace round and around, just as he had at the kingdom gates. "Bubbling blowfish," thought Gill with a gulp. "I'll never be able to avoid that in this state."

Then, just before Wham-Shell released the mace, the crustacean winked. His eyes had returned to their normal colour. Wham-Shell released the weapon, sending it careering towards the gem-eel cage. The wooden box splinted into a thousand pieces and the gem-eels were released.

"Noooooo!" Grimslobber cried as the gem-eels swarmed towards the diving bell. He jumped back, the Fish Master's Crown slipping from his head and clattering to the bell's metal floor. The Captain staggered forward and

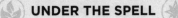

grimaced at the sound of something crunching beneath his feet. He raised his eyepatch and looked down in dismay. The Fish Master's Crown had been broken in two.

Instantly, the spell was broken. Hundreds of merfolk awoke from their nightmare and turned to face the Captain, furious at what he had done to them.

"Grimslobber, it's time you learned that Gillmen never give up!" cried Gill, recovering his water cannon. "Time to pay for your crimes."

"Time to skedaddle," spluttered the Captain, pressing down a lever at the back of the diving bell. As the furious merfolk looked on, the bell was winched up, smashing through the roof of the cave, back to the Fearsome Fang.

"He's getting away," hissed Prince Aquan, gnashing his teeth in frustration.

"Don't worry your royal dudeship," Zap said, slipping out from beneath the now dormant starfish. "Didn't you see who's gone along for the ride?"

Finella clapped her hands in excitement as she spotted what Zap was talking about. Gill Grunt had grabbed onto the bottom of the diving bell and was being hauled up after Grimslobber.

CHAPTER **THIRTEEN**

GRIMSLOBBER ESCAPES

"**H**aul me up!" Grimslobber yelled as the diving bell broke the surface of Deep Water Wasteland. "Haul me up, ye lice-infested bilge-swiggers."

The crew of the Fearsome Fang pulled and panted, manhandling the heavy device onto the deck.

"Cap'n, what happened?" asked Bonebeard as Grimslobber tumbled out of the bell.

"Mutiny," Grimslobber gurgled, shoving the remains of the crown into his satchel. "Mutiny, treachery and revolt. Those slovenly sea-dwellers will rue the day they were hatched, I tells thee. Once I've got them back under me spell I'll . . ."

"You'll what, dog-face?" The Pirates nearly fell over themselves as they span around. Gill Grunt was standing on top of the diving bell, his water cannon trained on Grimslobber. "I don't think you'll find they're so easy to control now, Captain."

"Ye scab-encrusted sea bass!" Grimslobber screamed. "I'll grill ye for me breakfast! I'll roast ye for me dinner! I'll barbecue ye for me supper! Ye'll never leave this ship alive."

"Brave words for a guy who's about to lose

a fight," smiled Gill, refusing to rise to the bait. All around him, the crew broke down into mocking laughter. "The Cap'n, lose?" jeered Bonebeard.

"What a joke!"

"Who's going to fight him anyways?" scoffed Squid-Ink.

"Not a little shrimp like ye," mocked Runtface. "Not with all of us at his side!"

Every pirate on the ship drew his weapon.

"Oh, you're right," agreed Gill, still looking down the barrel of his gun. "I couldn't beat you on my own . . ."

"So, ye be ready to surrender?" Grimslobber taunted, his own cutlasses in his paws. "Ready to walk me plank?"

Gill smiled. "But who said I was on my own anyway?"

The deck of the Fearsome Fang lurched, sending the pirates scurrying to starboard.

"It be an earthquake!" squeaked Runtface as he barrelled into the Captain.

The deck rolled the other way, pitching the pirates back to port.

"But we not be on any earth to quake, ye

129

salty swab," pointed out Squid-Ink, dropping his mortar gun.

The boat rocked back and forth. By now, most of the buccaneers were on their backs.

"What in Frightbeard's name is happening?" whined a dizzy Bonebeard.

"Why don't you look over the side and see?" called out Gill, enjoying the sight of the terrified pirates slipping this way and that.

"No!" shouted Grimslobber, clutching onto the steering wheel for dear life. "It can't be. It just can't be."

But it was. Every merperson the Captain had hypnotized had broken the surface and was rocking the Fearsome Fang, threatening to dump the entire crew into the churning water.

"Get on yer feet!" Grimslobber screamed at his men. "Man the cannons! Charge! Do something!"

"Did someone say charge?" Zap burst from the sea in a shower of white foam. Grimslobber

looked on helplessly as the water dragon soared over his head to land on the upper deck, electricity dancing around his open mouth. "Ride the lightning!"

"Hope you haven't started without me." Heavy feet thumped down on the lower deck as Wham-Shell joined the party. "Brace for the mace!"

"Is this the best ye can do?" Grimslobber bellowed, backing away despite his bluster.

"Not quite," replied Gill as a Portal opened above his head. With a roar, Spyro appeared in mid-air, smoke curling from his nostrils. "*This* is the best!"

"What are we waiting for, Gill?" Spyro called down. "I'm all fired up!"

Gill grinned at Grimslobber. "Battle stations!"

CHAPTER **FOURTEEN**

PIRATE BATTLE

The pirates didn't stand a chance. Disorientated from the merfolk's rocking, the bewildered buccaneers were left scrabbling for their scabbards and groping for their guns. Everywhere they turned they came face-to-face with a Skylander.

Zap giggled wildly as he slid across deck on a stream of slick sea slime, shocking pirates left, right and centre. Spyro swept down from above, butting them overboard. Wham-Shell smothered them in sticky starfish. And Gill sent them sprawling with jets of salty seawater from

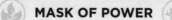
his cannon.

"I've had enough of this," yelped Runtface, jumping over the side of the ship. "Women and cowards first!"

"Wait for me," called Squid-Ink, diving away from the battle.

"I never wanted to be a pirate anyway," yelped Bonebeard, holding his nose and plunging overboard. "Yer on yer own, Cap'n!"

Grimslobber *was* on his own. His entire crew had either been dumped in the drink or had chosen to abandon ship. Even his parrots had flown the coup. With cutlasses a quiver, he tottered back on his two wooden legs, desperate to get away from the Skylanders.

As the Captain retreated, Spyro touched down beside Gill and the others. They didn't say a word – just advanced on Grimslobber step by step.

"Now then, mates," the Captain said as he inched back. He was on the plank now, shuffling

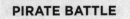

back as far as he could go. "Let's not be hasty lads. We can cut a deal. I has treasure hidden all over Skylands. Let me go and I'll share it with ye, on me grandmother's honour."

"People say that you sold your grandmother, Grimslobber . . ." Spyro said, never taking his eyes off the Captain.

"To pay for your first gold tooth," added Zap.

"Lies, all lies," whimpered Grimslobber, throwing his swords down and raising his hands in surrender. "Alright, it was me second gold tooth actually, but that's not important right now."

"What's important is that you enslaved all those merpeople," Gill said, no longer smiling. "And turned me against my friends."

"I admits that was a little hasty," Grimslobber pleaded, reaching inside his coat. "But I've learned me lesson. I'll turn over a new leaf, I promise ye."

"You will?" Gill stopped. Could the Captain

 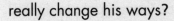

really change his ways?

"Yeah, next time I'll filet yer while I have the chance!" Grimslobber pulled out his hand, revealing the pistol he now held in his paw, a pistol pointing straight at Gill. "Say goodbye to your shipmates, Skylander!"

Grimslobber pulled the trigger but the shot went wide, flying harmlessly over Gill's head. The entire boat had tilted, pitched back by Prince Aquan and his mermen below. The Captain tottered back on the plank, his arms desperately wheeling, before finally tumbling over the side.

"Help!" he screamed. "I can't swim!"

Gill ran forward to catch the plummeting pirate, but it was too late. Grimslobber tumbled back, falling from the plank. But before the Captain could even hit the water, the Cloud Kraken exploded from the depths, opening its monstrous jaws wide and swallowing him whole. With a bellow of satisfaction, the great beast disappeared beneath the waves.

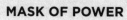

"Quick," said Zap, as the merpeople righted the ship. "We need to find that crown. Something that powerful has to be the Water fragment."

"You don't say," said a voice that stopped the Skylanders in their tracks.

Spyro hissed as he saw who was standing on the upper deck. "Kaos!"

"Ahoy there, SKYLOSERS," the evil Portal Master jeered. He had Captain Grimslobber's hat on his head and one half of the Fish Master's Crown in his hand. "Thank you for getting rid of that fool, Grimslobber. You saved me the trouble of sending him to his DOOOOOM! It's just a shame this thing got broken. It'll never enslave anyone again."

"Drop it Kaos," warned Gill, "before we drop you."

Kaos threw back his head and laughed.

138

"You dare threaten meeeee?" A storm cloud appeared above the Skylanders' heads. "I – Kaos – summon my TERRIBLE TORRENT OF TEMPESTUOUS TROUT! HA HA HA HAAAA!"

With a flash of lightning, fish reigned down from the cloud, smothering the Skylanders in a pile of flapping fins and snapping mouths. Kaos was nearly beside himself, giggling as his mortal enemies slipped and stumbled under the fishy downpour.

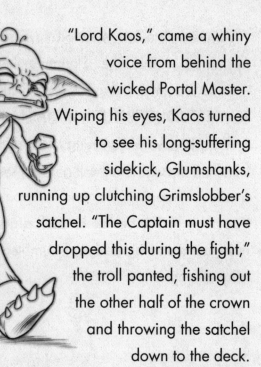

"Lord Kaos," came a whiny voice from behind the wicked Portal Master. Wiping his eyes, Kaos turned to see his long-suffering sidekick, Glumshanks, running up clutching Grimslobber's satchel. "The Captain must have dropped this during the fight," the troll panted, fishing out the other half of the crown and throwing the satchel down to the deck.

"At last," Kaos crowed, snatching it from Glumshanks' hands without as much as a thank you. "Behold . . . THE WATER FRAGMENT!"

With the Portal Master distracted, the unnatural shower of fish had subsided. As his friends dug themselves out, Gill Grunt was frantically trying to clear the trout that were bunging up his water cannon. All he needed was one shot.

Shrieking in triumph, Kaos turned to face the Skylanders. "The Mask of Power will be mine, all mine! And you," Kaos pointed a stubby finger at Gill, "will be DOOOOOOMED." A bolt of light flashed from the Portal Master's finger and smashed through the deck at Gill's feet.

"Oops," Kaos cackled, tucking the crown beneath his robes. "It looks like you've sprung a leak. I hope you can swim! Ha ha ha ha HAAAAAAAAAAA!"

The ship pitched to the side, but this time it wasn't anything to do with the merpeople. Water was gushing through the hole in the deck. They were taking on water.

"Lord Kaos?" Glumshanks whined, wringing his hands together.

"Yes, what is it?" snapped Kaos. "Can't you see I'm gloating?"

"Perhaps you can gloat on dry land? We're going down with the ship."

Kaos looked at his feet. The troll was right. The cold water was already up to his ankles.

"Good point. Happy sinking, FOOOOOOLS!"

Kaos clicked his fingers and in a flash of light they were gone.

"Let's get off this ship before she goes down," Zap yelled, shaking the last of the trout from his back.

"I've already called for a Portal," Spyro replied.

"Thanks for your help, your majesties," Wham-

Shell called to Aquan and Finella as the Portal appeared above their heads. Grabbing his mace, he leapt into the light, followed by Zap.

Gill, meanwhile, was running back across the slippery deck.

"What are you doing?" Spyro cried out, flying into the Portal. "Let's get out of here. Kaos has the fragment."

"I'm not so sure," Gill shouted back, scooping up Grimslobber's satchel. "There's something I need to check."

Clutching the bag to his chest, Gill flashed a fishy grin at Aquan and Finella, then jumped after Spyro.

In the water, the merpeople cheered as the Fearsome Fang sank without a trace.

CHAPTER FIFTEEN

THE WATER FRAGMENT

"I can't believe that Kaos got away with the water fragment," Zap grumbled, as they trudged to meet Eon in the Eternal Archive's vault. "That's totally, utterly bogus."

Spyro shook his head. "You're right, Zap, especially after all you went through."

"I'm sorry, Master." Wham-Shell looked up at Eon, despair written all over his face. "We failed you."

Eon stroked his white beard thoughtfully. "What about you, Gill? Do you think the mission was a failure?"

Gill rummaged in Grimslobber's satchel, drawing out a dirty old rag. "I'm not sure," he replied, dropping the bag to the floor. "At the beginning of all of this, you said that the Water fragment was hidden in something the complete opposite to its true nature."

"Indeed I did," the Portal Master smiled.

"At first I thought it must be the Fish Master's Crown, something that could control creatures who live in the water . . .

". . . but now you're not so sure?"

Gill reached into his belt and drew out the scrap of paper Eon had ripped from the Book of Power.

"What have you got there, Gill?" asked Spyro.

"It's the rag that Grimslobber used to wrap up the crown in his satchel," Gill explained.

"What did you want with that dirty old thing?" Wham-Shell asked.

"You're right," Gill agreed, lifting the paper

to meet the cloth. "It is filthy – the complete opposite of lovely clean water."

The paper began to glow, faintly at first but then so fiercely that they were all forced to turn away.

"The rag is the Water fragment," Gill announced as the cloth floated out of his hands and up into the air.

"Then Kaos –" began Spyro.

"Has stolen nothing more than a worthless, broken crown!" completed Zap. "Rad."

"Rad indeed," the Portal Master said, raising his palm. In a flash the rag was gone, replaced with a fragment of the Mask of Power. The Skylanders gasped as Eon plucked it from the air, turning the segment over in his hand.

"This fragment will be kept safe here in the vault," he said. "But this is all far from over."

Spyro nodded gravely. "Gillmen aren't the only ones who never give up. Kaos will be after the other fragments."

"There's one thing I still don't get," said Zap. "He hasn't got the Book of Power. How did he know where the Water fragment would be?"

"I don't know," Gill said, placing a friendly hand on the water dragon's shoulder. "But there is one thing I am sure of."

"What's that, Gill?" asked Spyro.

"Wherever Kaos goes next, the Skylanders will be waiting for him!"

To be continued in . . .

LIGHTNING ROD
FACES THE CYCLOPS QUEEN

LIGHTNING ROD

FACES THE
CYCLOPS QUEEN

CHAPTER ONE

THE STORM GIANT GAMES

"**L**adies and Gentlemen, we are proud to present the greatest champion Skylands has ever known – Lightning Rod!"

The crowd went wild as soon as Lightning Rod's name was announced. They cheered; they clapped; they threw their hats in the air. A couple of Rotting Robbies even threw their heads in the air, but the less said about that the better. Lightning Rod was the most popular contestant in the annual Storm Titan Games. In fact, some said he was the most popular contestant in the event's entire history. No one had won as many

 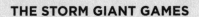

medals as he had, and no one had anywhere near as many statues carved in their image. They were everywhere you looked: Rod throwing a lightning bolt; Rod running a marathon; Rod lifting an entire herd of sabre-tusked elephants stacked on top of each other. There was even a statue of Rod snoring his beard off. Even when asleep, Rod was the most impressive specimen for miles around. No one performed like Rod, no one flexed their muscles like Rod, and no one polished off as many eggs for breakfast as Rod.

In the crowd, Pop Fizz bounced up and down in his seat as everyone's favourite Storm Titan made his way into the arena.

"Hey, watch it!" said Cali, as the excitable alchemist slopped potion all over her. "You're spilling that stuff everywhere!"

"Whoops, sorry," apologized Pop Fizz, before taking a slug from the bottle. There was a puff of smoke and the distinct whiff of

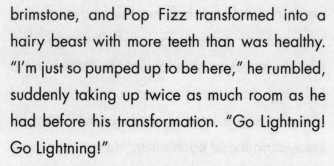
brimstone, and Pop Fizz transformed into a hairy beast with more teeth than was healthy. "I'm just so pumped up to be here," he rumbled, suddenly taking up twice as much room as he had before his transformation. "Go Lightning! Go Lightning!"

"Stop moving," snapped Drobot from the other side of Pop Fizz. "You are interfering with my visual circuits!"

With a gurgle, Pop Fizz shrunk back to his normal size.

"Whoops again," he spluttered, his eyes spinning from the sudden metamorphosis. "This is exciting though, isn't it? I mean, look at this place."

Drobot had to admit that the arena was spectacular. Over a billion Games had been played here, and every year the Storm Titans added on another new stand. It now stretched for miles and seated millions of spectators, all of whom were now looking expectantly at

Lightning Rod. The brilliant blue hero stood in the middle of the field, soaking up the applause, flexing his bulging muscles and flashing a blinding smile.

Cali was grinning too. Rod was in his element here, surrounded by his adoring fans. Yes, she knew that he loved being a Skylander, protecting the magical realm of Skylands from the forces of Darkness, but he was also massively proud of his sporting accomplishments. They all were.

"Do you think he's going to do it?" Pop Fizz asked, half-raising the soda bottle to his lips before being stopped by Drobot. "Do you think he's going to break the record?"

"There is a ninety-nine point nine nine nine per cent probability that Rod will triumph."

"Eh?" said Pop Fizz, looking completely bewildered.

"He said yes," whispered Cali as a hush fell over the crowd.

In the royal box, the King of the Storm Titans

had raised his hands. "My friends," he boomed, his voice like a thousand thunderstorms rolled into one. "Please be silent for our guest of honour."

Beside the king stood a tall thin man, leaning heavily on a crystal-topped staff. It was Eon, Skylands' greatest Portal Master. Eon had been asked to open this year's Games, but he looked so old, so tired. Cali frowned. She knew the last few weeks had been a trial for the ancient wizard, but she'd hoped the excitement of the Games would revive him. Still, the Portal Master smiled as he drew himself up, his eyes resting on Lightning Rod far below.

"People of Skylands," Eon said, his voice magically amplified around the stadium. "It is my pleasure to pronounce these Games . . . open."

A buzz of excitement rippled around the assembled throng. "And without further ado, we shall enjoy the first event – the five-hundred ton hammer throw. And our first contender, Lightning Rod!"

The crowd roared once again as Lightning Rod approached the massive metal ball and chain at the centre of the field. It was twice the size of the Titan, and yet he grabbed the heavy chain without hesitation. Taking the strain, he began to spin the ball round, faster and faster, electricity crackling up and down the metal links.

Cali couldn't help but be impressed. She often worked with the Skylanders, training them to use their powers, but she'd never seen Lightning Rod lift something this heavy, let alone spin it round.

"He's gonna win," Pop Fizz was babbling, almost beside himself. "He's gonna get the gold. I just know it."

But Drobot didn't comment.

Cali turned and saw he wasn't looking at Lightning Rod, but into the sky.

"What's wrong?" she asked, the fur on the back of her neck bristling.

"That is wrong," Drobot replied, pointing towards the clouds with a claw. Cali turned to see a solitary balloon drifting high above them. "If Lightning Rod lets go of the hammer . . ."

Cali didn't need him to complete the sentence. Worst of all, she knew who owned the balloon.

It was Flynn, the so-called best pilot in all of Skylands, and someone who seemed to have a knack for flying into trouble. The guy had an ego the size of an entire island, but he'd helped the Skylanders time and time again.

"We've got to warn them!" Cali cried out.

"Too late," reported Drobot as the Storm Titan let go of the chain and flung the hammer into the air. It rocketed up, soaring over the heads of the crowd . . . and zoomed straight for Flynn's balloon.

Can Lightning Rod save Flynn? Will the Skylanders stop Kaos from discovering the Air fragment of the Mask of Power? And who is the traitor in their midst?

Find out all this and more in . . .

LIGHTNING ROD
FACES THE CYCLOPS QUEEN

HEAD TO HEAD

Which Skylanders hero do you like best – the gallant Gillman or the wily water dragon?

GILL GRUNT

ROUND 1: ORIGINS

Growing up in the volcanic glass city of the Gillmen, Gill Grunt always knew he wanted to serve in the Gillmen Marines. As soon as he was old enough he enlisted and left the safety of his home to start training. He soon rose through the ranks, gaining a reputation for being a courageous sea soldier – even though a romantic heart still beat in his chest.

ROUND 2: BATTLE CRY

Fear the Fish!

ROUND 3: PERSONALITY

Brave and courageous, Gill is a loyal friend to have at your side. Protective and determined, Gill is a big-hearted Gillman who never, ever gives up.

ROUND 4: WEAPONS

Gill's water cannon can soak any enemy, and they know not to hang around when he loads his harpoons!

ROUND 5: SPECIAL ABILITIES

Gill can transform his water barrel into a jet pack to become a flying fish.

TOTAL:

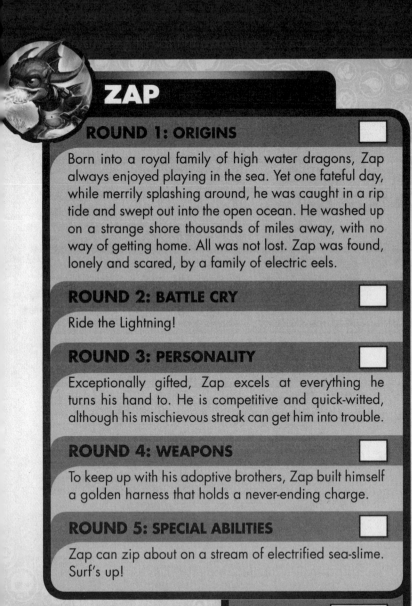

ZAP

ROUND 1: ORIGINS

Born into a royal family of high water dragons, Zap always enjoyed playing in the sea. Yet one fateful day, while merrily splashing around, he was caught in a rip tide and swept out into the open ocean. He washed up on a strange shore thousands of miles away, with no way of getting home. All was not lost. Zap was found, lonely and scared, by a family of electric eels.

ROUND 2: BATTLE CRY

Ride the Lightning!

ROUND 3: PERSONALITY

Exceptionally gifted, Zap excels at everything he turns his hand to. He is competitive and quick-witted, although his mischievous streak can get him into trouble.

ROUND 4: WEAPONS

To keep up with his adoptive brothers, Zap built himself a golden harness that holds a never-ending charge.

ROUND 5: SPECIAL ABILITIES

Zap can zip about on a stream of electrified sea-slime. Surf's up!

TOTAL:

Also available:

SKYLANDERS GIANTS
PORTAL OF PUZZLES STICKER BOOK

ONK BEAKMAN

SKYLANDERS SPYRO'S ADVENTURE
THE MACHINE OF DOOM

SKYLANDERS UNIVERSE
QUIZ QUEST
QUIZ AND ACTIVITY BOOK

SKYLANDERS UNIVERSE
MAGIC & TECH
BOOK OF ELEMENTS

SKYLANDERS UNIVERSE
FIRE & WATER
BOOK OF ELEMENTS